Number

Dorling Kinderlsey
www.dk.com

Editor Fiona Munro
Designer Lisa Hollis

Published in Great Britain in 1997
by Dorling Kindersley Limited, 9 Henrietta St, London WC2E 8PS
This edition published in 2000

A CIP catalogue record for this book is available from the British Library.

ISBN 0-7513-6704-4

Color reproduction by DOT Gradations
Printed in Hong Kong by Wing King Tong

Number Four

COLIN AND JACQUI HAWKINS

Dorling Kindersley

"I like to know everything," said Number Four.

Hello, I'm Number Four !

He was a very nosey Numberlie.
Number Four lived in the fourth house in
Numbertown. It was a pink house with four
red windows and four pink chimney-pots.
The address was 4, Number Lane.

Inside Number Four's house there was a very old four-poster bed.

This is cosy.

What's that?

There were also four telescopes. Nosey Number Four liked to see everything that was going on in Numbertown.

He also had four televisions so that he could keep up with all the Numberlie news.

What's the news?

Every week, Number Four borrowed four books from the library.

I like stories.

"I want to know more!" said Number Four.

Every day at four o'clock, Number Four
made four cups of tea with four tea-bags.
He also ate four jam doughnuts.
"I wonder where tea-bags grow?" he said.
"I wonder how the jam gets
into the doughnuts?"

"I want to know more!"
said Number Four.

Every day, Number Four went around
Numbertown poking his nose
into everything. One day, he saw that
Number Five had a new garden shed.
Number Four opened the door.

"I want to know more!"
said Number Four.

CRASH!
CRASH!
CRASH!
CRASH!

Everything fell out on top of Number Four!

One windy day, the wind whistled around Number Four's chimney.

Whoooo!

"Who's there?" asked Number Four.

Who's there?

"Who's there, there, there, there . . ." echoed the chimney.

Whoooosh!

Great clouds of black soot shot down the chimney and all over Number Four. It took him four hours to sweep up.

When Number Four was shopping
one morning, he saw Number Three
getting on the Numbertown bus.
"Where are you going?" he asked.
"Wait for me!"

Number Three laughed and waved.
"Mind your own business,
you nosey number!"

The yellow bus drove away.

As he walked along, Number Four saw some
bees buzzing around their hive.
"I wonder how bees make honey?"
he thought, as he looked inside.

"I want to know more!"
said Number Four.

What's in here?

Buzz! Buzz!
Buzz! Buzz!

"Buzz off, you
nosey Numberlie!"
buzzed the bees angrily, and they chased
him all the way back to Numbertown.

Later, as Number
Four was walking
past Number Three's
house, he saw an
open window.
"I know he's out,"
said Number Four.
"I'll just have a quick peep." He poked his
nosey nose through the window.
"Oh no!" he said. "Looks like trouble!"

Splash! Splash! Splash! Splash!

There was water everywhere!
Number Three, who was very forgetful,
had forgotten to turn off the taps.

Number Four waded into the house and
turned off the taps in the bathroom.
He cleared up the water with four mops,
four sponges and four buckets.
"This is a clean-up job!" he said.

When Number Three arrived home,
Number Four told him the
whole, soggy story.
"I'm glad you're a nosey Numberlie!"
said a very pleased Number Three.

At four o'clock, in the Numbertown cafe,
Number Three thanked

Number Four.
They had four
milkshakes,
then four jam
doughnuts.
"Does anyone know how the jam gets
in the middle?" asked Number Four.
The other Numberlies all
shook their heads and laughed.

"He wants to know **more**,
that Number Four!"

What a nosey Numberlie!